Also by J.N. Macawell

Grim Kid
Grim kid new world order
Grim Kid: Son Of The Grim Reaper

Grim kid stories
Aidan The Devil's Cambion : A Grim Kid Story
Woe Of The Nephilim
ADONIJAH : A Grim Kid story

Mythical tales
Moonlit A Werewolf's Tale
Broomstick a witch's tale

The Abaddon Chronicles
1692

The Genova chronicles
The Genova Chronicles : Goddess Of The Moon

Wizards and Genies
Wizards And Genies: The Prince Of Arevesa

Standalone
Seasick A Merman's Tale Part 1
The Lycanthrope Confessions
The Skinwalker
The Snow Queen By J.N. Macawell
SeaSick A merman's Tale part 2
Stumpp The Werewolf Of Bedburg
Reaper An Angel's Tale
The skudakumooch
Star Child

Table of Contents

Dedicated to

Jalen, Heather and Divine

For your continuous belief in me . Keep rocking on

The Genova Chronicles: Goddess Of The Moon
By J.N. Macawell

PART ONE: The witch And The Werewolf

CHAPTER 1

GENOVA SAT ON THE BANKS of the river Laírasan that ran through the woods near the village of the same name. Her brown hair ran down her Shoulders sticking out of the hood of the brown cloak that covered her head in the dim light of dusk. Genvoa was a beautiful young maiden with soft brown skin and sparkling hazel eyes. She waited for her friend Edmund to come and let his herd of Sheep drink from the river before she followed him to lush Green hills just beyond the patch of trees Genova sat in . The end of her light blue frock laid upon the green grass as she picked the flowers and pulled up the grass of the forest floor. Her necklace rested on her chest as she lifted her hand, taking the Blue crescent moon shaped sapphire and gripping it.

THE SKY WAS LEFT IN an orangish pink twilight when Genova stood up and looked to the trees in the distance as three Sheep made their way towards the stream. The sheep looked at Genova as a little lamb limped its way to the river joining its Mother at her scrawny legs. Edumd Walked from the trees looking at Genova with a smile on his face. Edmund was a rather skinny boy with a head of shaggy Brown hair that fell before light brown eyes. Though he was the son of the renowned Marchioness dé Laírasan he hadn't come of the age where the title of Marquis was bestowed upon him. He spent his nights watching the herd of Sheep and talking to Genova who was the daughter of a Marchioness who fled to the village of Gévaudan when Genova was a newborn. Claiming the teritory as her new feifdom.

Genova walked across the small stream of water slightly lifting her dress so that she didn't get the expensive frock wet. Edmund opened his arms as Genova rushed across the water and threw her arms around the young Marquis. It had been a week since she had seen him last and she was only happy to wait for him when he asked her to .

Genova would never admit it but she harbored a great affinity for Edmund but she knew he saw her as more of a sister than a lover.

"Did you bring it ?" Asks Genova.

Edmund reached into the brown leather satchel and pulled out an envelope sealed with the wax crest of the Fawcett family on it. The old English F had been their symbol since the thirteen hundreds and it was easily recognizable.

"I brought you something better than an old book, an invitation to my wedding!" Says Edmund handing the envelope to Genova who looked at it trying to fight her tears..

"You're marrying someone ?" Asks Genova .

"She's a dutchess. I want you to meet her !" Answers Edmund.

Genova forced herself to smile and nod her head; it was all she could bring herself to do . She remembered the first day she met Edmund. They were only seven years old and the girls in the village had all run off to the market place to buy dresses. Genova was a rather peculiar child in the eyes of the other village girl, she spent her Time in The forest looking at the trees and playing with sticks as if they were swords. It wasn't until Edmund had run from a group of boys that were tossing rocks at him that Genova had even noticed him and fought them away with a slender stick that they became inseparable.

More sheep came to drink from the water as Genova opened the envelope Reading the handwritten letter that was inside. The date of the wedding was February third 1761 . It was only a week from the very day. Genova looked at the letter and felt her heart breaking inside her chest as she folded the paper putting it back into the envelope . She had to be happy for Edmund because he was finally going to be cementing his status as Marquis by marrying the dutchess who apparently was named Inés Dé Féaran.

"I'm happy for you !" Says Genova swallowing every bit of her sadness as she closed the envelope pressing the wax seal with her thumb.

"Are we going to the hilltops?" Asks Genova.

"I have to be back home in an hour so I can be there for the banquet tonight so I don't think I am going to be able to take the sheep tonight to the hills today !" Says Edmund

Genova knew that was where her mother was going to be and why she had to sneak out to get to the river . It was a preparation for the wedding and Genova couldn't bear to go and fake a smile . She didn't want to see the soon to be bride or the groom she had hoped would be hers one day .

Genova crossed the river looking back at Edmund as she reached the other side. As she walked away her tears forced themselves out . Edmund looked at the sheep drinking the water of the river as Genova faded from view; he was quite happy . He was going to be married soon and a year after he would inherit the entire Fawcét estate and the title of Marquis Dé Laírasan. He would be the most wealthy man in the entire region.

GENOVA WALKED PAST the edge of the woods looking to the beggars outside the Crafted crown tavern. The old tavern was never empty and the sounds of the signing barmaid filled the air . The beggars looked at Genova as she passed by , Their faces were stained with dirt and Their clothes had holes ripped into them . Genova looked at the beggars as the mother smiled at her. Genova had given them enough money to get meals many times . The two children shared a piece of bread the mother had bought with Genova's last generous donation.

The sun had set, leaving the sky in darkness as Genova passed by the tavern and looked at the store front of the tailor's shop that was still open. A tall woman who looked just a few years older than Genova stood getting a dress tailored . She had long black hair and bright blue eyes that looked out the window as she stood on the small circular stool as the tailor put the finishing touches on the white dress. It looked more expensive than Genova's entire house cost . It was made from a beautiful white silk and embroidered with golden thread at the breasts and stomach . The train of the dress trailed behind her on the ground.

"Madam I've finally done it, you are going to be the best dressed bride in all of france !" Says the tailor as he got off his knees and admired his work.

"Really I don't feel like it, I feel like something is missing !" Answers the future bride.

Genova had no way of knowing that the woman standing before her in the shop was the duchess that Edmund was going to be marrying in one week's time.

"What could be missing madam, surely you are mistaken !" Says the tailor.

The tailor was a rather scrawny man with a head of white hair and a pair of spectacles that hung at the end of his nose. He was dressed in a light blue button up shirt and a pair of formal dress pants.Genova looked at the woman as she looked at her stepping down from the stool and Opened the door of the shop.

"Can I help you ?' asks Inés .

"No, I was just looking at your beautiful dress!" Says Genova.

"WELL THIS IS A PRIVATE matter if you don't mind!" Says Inés Rolling her eyes at Genova.

Genova walked away from the young dutchess and made her way towards the small houses with thatched roofs as the torches were lit in the marketplace lighting up the closed storefronts and little houses. Genova lived at the edge of the small town in a large house made of stone with stained glass windows and a black gate of iron that bordered the hillsides . The shelsmyer mansion was truly a marvel to behold. Genova pushed open the gates which met each forming a Plaque in the center where a metallic S sat when the two doors joined together. The maid opened the door as Genova walked up the steps.

"Your Mother has requested your presence in the parlor!" Says the maid .

She was a beautiful girl with a caramel skin tone and a head of reddish brown hair that curled down her back. Genova had been confined to the maid many times and yet she still forgot her name which was Megerah. Genova walked past the main room of the house towards the parlor which was a small room under the grand staircase that greeted those who walked in at the door. Genova pushed through the red curtains and walked into the room. The smells of sweet cinnamon Incense and candle wax.

Her mother sat with two of her coven sisters at the large wooden table topped with burning candles and beautiful baskets filled with delicious fruits and pinecones. Genova's mother Zerah shelsmyer was a beautiful woman only thirty years in age . She had long brown hair and a pair of brown eyes that looked at Genova with disgust.

"You are a rather scrawny young woman aren't you ?' Asks Zerah.

"Did you call me here to insult me in front of your coven sisters ?" Protests Genova.

"Take a seat child !" Says Helinore who was a rather pudgy soothsayer.

She wore her blonde hair in a bun above her head. She had on a beautiful gown made of green velvet and a crown of leaves sat upon her head. Genova sat at the table before the three witches in the dimly lit room . four candles lit and it was hardly enough to light the table let alone the entire room.

"Have you experienced any odd feelings lately dear child?"
Asks Zerah.

"No I have not'!' answers Genova.

It was a question Genova had been asked more than enough
times just because her sister had been born with magic. It was
no secret to the coven that Genova was as they described as
a pitiful mortal . Genova wasn't even sure she wanted to be
a witch; she had seen what it had turned her sister into the
once vibrant and happy girl had turned into a reclusive and
unhappily married crone. Though she wasn't old or ugly her
personality had changed drastically . Her mother had always
been that way hovering over Genova every second reminding
her that if something magical happened to her to tell her
immediately.

'You're coming to an age where your powers should be
blooming beautifully !' says Gringin.

Gringin was by far the most beautiful of the three elder
witches with smooth colored skin that rivaled even the purest
chocolate. Her eyes were a heavenly shade of blue and a smile
that was ever contagious. She set a book with a ripped leather
cover and old faded pages.

"Do you know what this is ?" Asks Gringin

" uh An old book!' answers Genova, lifting an eyebrow in
confusion.

"'Not just any old book, the book of Valarheyian prophecy.
Do you remember the story your mother used to tell you about
The light of Valarhey?' Askew Zerah

"You mean the princess the faun king gave to a coven of old
shelsmyer witches ?" Asks Genova.

"Well I wouldn't say they were old !" Laughs Helinore.

"Take a look at what the princess looks like in the book of Valarheyian Prophecy!" Says Gringin.

sliding the book across the table to Genova on a page that had two drawings on both sides. The one on the left was a baby wrapped in linen with the same necklace that Genova had on her neck. Under the drawing was a paragraph that read .

"And she was sent from the dimension of the Ferahogan system unto the milky way where she was handed to the only group of humans who kept Saren's order, even though Azvaskae had kept the great faun king and all the Gods of light held captive . The elder fauns escaped and gave her the gift her father had given her a necklace of fine sapphire shaped like the crescent moon for it was what she embodied. She was the spirit of the moon, a living body who in death would be it's face. the last bit of hope Valarhey had left rested with the Goddess of the moon!'

Genova looked at the picture to the right where a hand-drawn ink picture of her sat on the page. Genova looked at the drawing of the maiden that stood in the forest. with a brown hood on her head and a sword in her hands .

She looked to the paragraph and it read

"In her sixteenth year the child would begin to display unimaginable power it is in this time she would be taken from her village and sent to the village of Dolé to harness her gifts only after she does so could she ever be strong enough to face her cousin Azvaskae the fallen Goddess of Valarhey and queen of the Gods of Glourhaven . The road to restoring Valarhey is a shaky and uncertain one but she shall come in the name of shelsmyer sent forth with a blade of steel. in her final hour Azvaskae shall have won and the moon Goddess reborn

She shall take her head and the Serpent of Galvaneller would finally be Dead. !"

Genova wanted to keep reading but the rest of the page had been ripped from the book leaving her baffled and anxious to read on .

"You think that is me ?" Laughs Genova.

"We know it is !" Says Zerah.

"I'm not a faun how can I be the daughter of the faun king!" Genova points out.

"Valarheyian Goddesses are born with human legs no Matter who their parents are!" Says Helinore.

"Well If that was me, where are my powers? I'm almost eighteen and still I haven't displayed unimaginable power!" Says Genova taking a piece from the passage she had just read to make her point.

She didn't even know anything about the religion of valarheyianism nor did she care . She was much too worried about the consequences of practicing any form of witchcraft to even look at a book of Valarheyian spells or focus her attention on making a proper potion. It was a sure way to get her tortured and sent to the stake.

"Oh one more thing before you go I'm going to need you to get ready. We have a banquet at the Fawcét Mansion we have to go to !" Says Zerah

Genova was afraid her mother would say she had to attend the banquet and have to see who the lucky bride was.

On the other side of a large village Edmund closed the sheep into their pasture behind the stables of the red barn where the horses grazed on the fresh hay that Edmund had given them .

He took the lantern off the wall of the barn as he walked inside, checked on the horses and walked to the back of the large house that should soon be his. He walked into the back door letting the smells of freshly cooked chicken and boiled potatoes fill the air outside.

He passed through the kitchen as the maids and manservants made their in and out of the kitchen setting the table that would seat more than fifty-seven guests tonight

The fireplace roared behind the large seat at the end of the table that resembled a throne.

Edmund took a seat as Inés walked into the room wearing the newly tailored dress she had just been given.

"Do you like it ?" Asks Inés .

Edmund looked at his future bride with eyes of astonishment as she took a seat next to him and placed her hand on the back of his palm that sat on the table.

"I do !" Says Edmund looking at Inés.

"You told me you wanted me to someone tonight her name was Genevieve right ?" Asks Inés

"It's Genova!" Says Edmund.

"That's what I said isn't it ?" Laughs Inés.

Edmund felt his heart racing as Inés stood up and united the strings of his cloak, taking the brown wool covering off his white linen shirt and placing her hand on his partially exposed chest.

"As long as you know I am the most important woman in your life I'll be fine with meeting her !" Says Inés kissing Edmund on the cheek and walking out of the room.

Edmund felt like everything was falling into place. In one week he would be married and eventually be the father of a child or two and he would have no one to tell him what to use his money on. He was the king of his own fate. All he had to do was go through with all the arrangements that were taken care of by his Aunt. He would be able to live up to the status that his mother had created for the Fawcét name before she left him in a basket in the woods to beasts of the forest. Everything started with how well things went tonight the Fawcét name would finally be restored and Edmund would be to thank for it .As long as fate stayed on his side but as history has told us time and Then again fate has a mind of Its own.

Chapter 2

GENOVA LOOKED OUT THE window of the carriage as the book of Valarheyian prophecy sat on her lap that was covered by the purple velvet dress she wore. The sleeves nearly hit the leather cover of the book. Her mother looked at her with a distasteful stare as she slouched her Shoulders.

"Don't slouch dear, a lady without perfect poise is hardly a lady at all !" Says Zerah.

Genova looked at her mother as the carriage came to a halt in front of the towering mansion . The coachman opened the door and Genova slid out waiting in line to for her turn to enter the house. Genova couldn't see into the door but she could smell the food that had been prepared and heard the notes of a finely tuned violin coming from inside. The sounds of laughter became more audible as the line quickly died down . Zerah and Genova approached the door as she was greeted by a man dressed in a neat brown tuxedo. A curled mustache sat on his face as he looked at Genova.

"Your name and title please!" Says the man .

"Genova shelsmyer I am the future Marchioness of Gévaudan !" says Genova

"Right this Way madam !" Says the man directing Genova to the dining hall.

Genova marveled at the large house; the rooftop of the bottom story rose high above her head and was lined with beautiful Floral arrangements. Banners barring the Fawcét crest of a wolf standing in its hind legs breathing fire hung from the high raised ceiling Genova walked into the dining room as the other guests took their seats.

"Wow .!" Says Genova looking at how many people sat at the one table.

The table had been topped with decadent cakes and desserts that sat alongside silver platters of exotic cheeses and breads. The centerpiece was the roasted pig with a delicious red apple lodged into its mouth. An ice swan sat next to it and a plate of chicken. It was truly a feast that Genova couldn't wait to end. She looked at Edmund who sat with a girl she had met just a few hours before at the tailor's shop.

"Genova over here!" Shouts Edmund as he beckons her closer with a wave of his hand.

Genova walked over to him, taking a seat on the opposite side in which Inés sat .

Genova looked at Inés who had changed out of her wedding dress and into a much more appropriate gown. The duchess looked at Genova With a stare Sharp enough to cut her .

"You're that girl who was looking in the window at the Tailor's shop!" Says Inés.

"You two have already met ?" Asks Edmund .

"You should try staying out of people's busInéss. It's looked down upon in sophisticated society!" Snaps Inés as she grabs Edmund's hand and laid her head on his shoulder.

Genova felt her chest growing heavy with anger as she felt the impact of Inés's insults Weighing on her. She didn't mean to offend her any way it was clear Inés felt Genovaa was a threat to her and Edmund's marriage. She had turned her nose at her before she even knew who she was Genova cared not about making friends with her. She knew that if they went on fighting Edmund would take her side and Genova would end up losing the only friend she truly had.

'What's so sophisticated about her she sounds like a snobbish brat!" Genova thought to herself as looked at her mother who sat next to Edmund's aunt on the other side of the table.

"Edmund tells me you can cook. Why didn't you help with the banquet?" Asks Inés .

"I didn't know about that there was a wedding until today let alone a banquet tonight!" Genova , trying to be as polite as she could.

Genova rolled up her sleeves as a servant came and filled the golden chalice in front of her with wine .The red wine was warm and Genova found the violet Red liquid quite appealing to look at .The Golden cup only made it more vibrant in contrast. Genova took notice of the old English F in the imprinting. The F stood for Fawcétt Genova knew that Edmund had big shoes to fill. The Fawcétt name was a gold mine to those who were born into it.it came with many strings attached however just as the Shelsmyer name did.

"Thank you!' says Genova.

"My pleasure madam !" Answer the servant.

Genova lifted the wine to her nose taking a quick sniff of the potent beverage before taking a sip.the taste of sour grapes filled her mouth as she set the cup back down.

Inés stood up and lifted chalice into the air

"I would like to propose a toast to the future Marquis and my future husband!" Says Inés .

Everyone sitting at the long table lifted their chalices into the air and drank the wine that had been poured inside.Edmund looked at Genova as she set her cup down and Inés walked into the kitchen leaving her alone . Genova took a piece of sweet bread off the plate in front of her and ripped a piece off, setting the rest of it on her plate.

"What do you think? she's great isn't she?" Asks Edmund.

"Yes, something special!" Says Genova with a smile.

She didn't know how long she could lie to Edmund she wanted him to be happy but at the rate things were going between her and Inés she came to realize she might not be in the picture for that much longer.she couldn't stand her and she knew she certainly didn't deserve anyone as incredibly wonderful as Edmund .

Edmund looked at Genova as a tear rolled down her eye and she wiped it away as fast as she could. She didn't want to make tonight about her it was Edmund's celebration and she had come to support him.

"What's wrong?" Asks Edmund.

"Nothing I just need to get some air !" Says Genova wiping her muoth with her napkin and fleeing into the kitchen

. Inés was sitting on the counter and drinking a bottle of wine. Genova rushed out the door and began weeping uncontrollably as fell to her knees .Her heart was broken . She couldn't stand to see Inés with Edmund; it had stirred something inside her that she couldn't explain. Something that felt so horrible she didn't want to acknowledge it and give it power over her. Genova lifted her head as the sapphire moon charm began to emit a bright green light .

Genova looked at the charm in confusion as she lifted it off her neck and a bright green beacon began to spiral into the air . Edmund Walked outside and Genova covered the necklace with her hands as he walked closer to her .

"What's wrong, why were you crying ?" Asks Edmund.

"I just needed some air, I'm fine!" says Genova, standing up and hiding the necklace behind her back.

Edmund looked at her unsure why she was acting so strange . He didn't understand her sometimes nor did he ever try to figure out why she did the things she does. He didn't want her to be out here to long because deep down he couldn't stand Inés either; he was hoping she would be able to help him get through the night without him trying to put himself out of his own misery. The only reason he had agreed to marry her was to solidify His title; she was just the unwanted bonus that came with it.

"Well when you are done getting air, please come back inside!". Says Edmund..

He walked back inside and Genova took the necklace from behind her back.

The green light once again shot out, spiraling into the air and finding rest among the clouds in the dark sky.

Zerah felt something telling her to go outside and check on Genova. She had been gone for quite some time . She stopped talking to Edmund's aunt who was a shelsmyer witch. She stood up and walked outside unsure why she had the feeling that Genova was in trouble.

She saw the green light rising high above the mesmerized sixteen year old as it lit the barn and the hillsides with the same light green color as the clouds that it touched. Zerah could see genvoa's eye glowing a florescent green. From the necklace came the voice of a woman who chanted in Valarheyian.

"Genova put the necklace down and come here!" Says Zerah.

She knew that the charm the faun king had placed on the necklace keeping her safe from her cousin Azvaskae had worn off . All this time Azvaskae had used her power to try and find the last bit of hope the Valarheyian Gods of the light had left . She had turned the necklace into a beacon so that she could find the young princess.

Genova was drawn to the green light. She didn't want to put it down; she wanted to stand right where she was and watch it spiral into the sky for as long as it burned bright.

Zerah snatched the necklace out of Genova's hand and tossed the necklace far beyond the pasture of sheep. The green light was put out once again and Genova was free from its hypnotizing clutches.

Far away from Laírasan in the forest of Gévaudan Azvaskae watched as the light died down . The Goddess looked at the witches that stood before the fire with a smile on her face as she took the pin, keeping her long black hair in a bun out of her head. Her Black hair fell to her shoulders as she looked into flames . The witches joined hands and looked to the fire as Azvaskae lifted her hands over the searing hot flame. Her hands glee with a black light as waves get hands over the fire as a puff of black smoke arose from the fire. In it she could see Genova sitting at the table next to Edmund once again.

"That's your cousin she doesn't look so harmful!" Laughs one of Azvaskae's witches .

"The ones who stand between a Goddess and Victory never do but you can't be fooled by her innocent appearance. That child is the last bit of light standing in my way! You know what we do to people who stand in my way don't you?" Asks Azvaskae.

"What about the charm that Saren placed on her ?" Asks Jink the youngest of the six witches that stood before Azvaskae.

"The charm has run its course, the necklace can no longer protect her, get ready and call forth your sisters, it's time we took a ride to visit my cousin!". Says Azvaskae.

She was by far the most beautiful creature anyone had ever seen with long black hair and light green eyes. she clothed herself in black garments of silk that trailed behind her lifting itself off the ground as the wind picked up Azvaskae's sister had already been made aware of her intentions for last light of Valarhey. Nersia was the holder of Earth's natural forces; she called herself mother nature . Her messenger owl perched itself on the branches above the witches who grabbed their brooms off the tree and prepared to take flight into the night. The large bird Opened its wings and flew through the air and sent a loud screeching hoot through the air .

Azvaskae's witches sat upon their brooms taking flight as the owl made its escape. Azvaskae grabbed her broom and sat upon it taking her Time she wanted to revel in the sorrow she was about to instill in the hearts of Shelsmyer coven and the entire Ferahogan system in which the kingdom of Valarhey stood .she had waited seventeen years to kill the Goddess foretold to be her undoing.

"To Laírasan ! we have a witch to kill !' shouts Azvaskae .

she flew over the field where the other witches of her coven sat around a fire . The sky was filled with a swarm of witches dressed in black flying in the clouds in the midst of a fine winter night . Azvasake made her way to the front of the flock of cackling witches.

"To victory we ride we'll find the girl at the Fawcétt mansion!" Shouts Azvaskae.

Her rule over the Ferahogan system was made official tonight the Goddess of the moon would die. She'd use the one thing strong enough to kill a Valarheyian God . A blade made of the primordial darkness manifested in metallic form. Galvianium was a foul substance that no longer had a grip over Azvaskae or the Gods of Glourhaven, but Genova could be killed with it.

Genova looked at Edmund who was drunk out of his mind and Inés who sat upon his lap as her family told him stories about her. Genova didn't care to pay attention to them; she was still more concerned about the necklace her mother had tossed into the grassy hills . Why did it emit such a light and why was she so entranced by it . If she was a witch her body and mind wouldn't find such things so odd and as most people would say evil.

Zerah waited outside the house for her coven sisters to join her; she had already blown the horn to call them. Gringin and Helinore Walked through the gates as Zerah got an eye full of the approaching witches.

"The necklace it's power is gone Azvaskae sent forth a homing beacon !" Says Zerah.

"Then we must send her to Dolé at once. The Werewolves are the only ones who can help her !" Says Gringin .

A ball of fire shot towards Helinore barely Missing her as the flying witches of Azvaskae's coven approached the Fawcét

Mansion. Zerah looked at the goddess as she landed in front of the gates.

"Make this easier on yourselves give me the daughter of Saren and I'll spare you!" Says Azvaskae.

Helinore and Gringin looked at Azasake as Zerah rushed into the house, closing the door behind her . She walked back into the dining hall to see the table had been moved and everyone had been dancing . Genova sat down on the same chair watching everyone enjoy the company of someone they held dear to them .

'Genova we have to go!" Says Zerah grabbing Genova by the sleeves and pulling her towards the kitchen.She moved her as far she could she knew the witches could only hold Azvaskae and her coven off for a few minutes.

"WHAT'S WRONG?" ASKS Genova Noticing the look of extreme distress in her mother's face .

"I'll explain later but right now we have to get out of here!"says Zerah opening the back door and letting Genova out of the house.

"She's over here !" Shouts one of the witches who had been circling the house.

"Whatever happens, run and don't stop !" Says Zerah as she hugged the little Goddess that she had raised. She looked at her and pointed to the woods not too far away from the house.

Genova rushed towards the pasture where the sheep had been grazing on the grass, hopping over the white fences and making a run for the open hills of countryside . She looked back as the three witches sent fire hurling at Zerah setting her body ablaze . Genova knew that she did have time to go back; she couldn't . Gringin rushed towards Genova as Azvaskae's witches flew towards her

"Go Genova !" Shouts Gringin as she neared the child who picked up the necklace as she passed the spot her mother had tossed it in.

She it back on her neck and made hast towards the towering pine trees of the forest

Azvaskae stood at the edge of the wood looking at her cousin as she made her way towards her.

The Goddess looked at her remembering the time she had stood this close to her victory.

It was sixteen years ago and the child was a mindless newborn. The necklace had burned the goddess when she tried to kill her . It gave the Zerah enough time to escape with the infant in hand . Genova fell upon the floor of the forest looking upon Azvaskae with anger as she killed her mother and had come to kill her as well.

gripping her necklace she stood up staring her in the eyes

"I'm not Afraid of you !" Says Genova.

"Of course you're not because of what you read in the book of Prophecy but I have a Prophecy for you. the necklace's power faded and the evil Goddess choked the life out of the Savior of Valarhey stabbing her in the chest with the same poisonous metal her father is entrapped by !" Says Azvaskae reaching into her garments pulling out a dagger made of a Galvainium.

Galvainium a metallic substance capable of killing even the strongest Valarheyian Gods or Goddesses.

Azvaskae grabbed Genova and a spark of green light ignited from the necklace forcing her into a pine tree that stood behind her . Genova ran into the forest keeping the necklace gripped tightly between her hands as she ran with her brown hair and purple sleeves trailing behind her in the wind.

"Don't just sit there, find her !" Shouted Azvaskae.

Genova rushed through the trees as the sounds of horse's' hooves pounding the rich soils of the forest echoed through the trees. Gringin stepped out of a carriage and Genova rushed towards her . Gringin stepped back into the carriage and slammed the door shut. with a loud crack of Helinore's whip the horses ran down the dirt paved path disappearing into the night.

Chapter 3

GENOVA OPENED HER EYES as the sun rose high above the trees Gringin sat with the book of Valarheyian prophecy wide open. The carriage was moving at a steady pace as Genova lifted her head off the glass of the window.

"Keep your necklace on at all times. I've renewed your father's charm so that Azvaskae can't find you !" Demands Gringin.

"IS MY MOTHER GOING to be okay?" Asks Genova.

''Zerah is no longer with us but do not fear child, your real mother is still alive waiting for you to defeat Azvaskae and set the gods of the light free !' Answers Gringin.

Genova looked out the window to the never ending sea of trees thinking about what awaited her . She knew she had no power; the closest thing to it she had came from the sapphire necklace that she wore. How was she going to defeat Azvaskae when she barely escaped with her life .

Edmund Opened his eyes, lifting his head off the table and standing up everyone had left after Zerah's scorched body was found outside . He could still picture the panic that I folded as the people left the mansion . Inés lay next to Edmund with her head resting comfortably in the back of her chair. The fireplace had turned to embers as Edmund looked out the window to the hills . He felt like something bad was coming. He didn't know what it was but the feeling manifested itself as negative thoughts about the wedding.

Genova's sister came with her husband to retrieve her mother's body . Unlike Genova, Scarlett was Zerah's legitimate daughter and the sight of her mother's crispy corpse brought tears to her face. Scarlett was much older than Genova; it was hard to believe they were sisters. She had a head of long brown hair and light brown eyes just like Zerah. She lifted her mother into the coffin that had been prepared for her and mounted her husband's horse as the three people who had come with her lifted the coffin and followed the horse to the front of the gate.Edmund rushed outside as fast as he could, stepping in front of the horse.

"What do you want, Edmund?" Asks Scarlett.

"Where is Genova? I sent Jasper to her house last night and she wasn't there ?" Asks Edmund

"I SENT HER TO FINISHING school if you want you can write her letters or something!' says Scarlett lying to the young Marquis as she wrapped her arms around her husband.

Her husband was a Marquis as well and they lived a days trek from Laírasan in the a much wealthier village . He was a soldier in the king's army and as such got more land than those who didn't fight . He was a slender gentleman with a head of blondd hair he had topped with a triangular shaped hat from which a single feather protruded.

Edmund opened the gate Letting the horse and the men carrying the coffin out as he looked to the front door to see Inés standing in front of it. He walked towards her as she sat on the first step of the porch and joined her.

"Why are you sad?" Asks Edmund.

"Why do you care so much about Genova when I am going to be your wife?" Asks Inés.

"SHE IS MY OLDEST AND dearest friend !" Answers Edmund.

"I understand !" Says Inés .

Genova looked at the page of the book of Valarheyian Prophecy that Gringin was reading .the picture looked like Edmund but it wasn't him because the picture depicted a Werewolf in mid shift . Genova would know if Edmund was a Werewolf.

"Who's that supposed to be ?" Asks Genova

"The eternal alpha of the Fawcét pack !" Answers Gringin.

Genova looked at Gringin not believing that she said Fawcét it was Edmund's last name .it had become a rather popular name

"What does it say ?" Asks

"In the darkest hour of our lost hope the Fawcét Alpha shall take his place as king of werewolves. Along with the Light Of valarhey. she will be set forth and slay evil after the wolf and the light have both been reborn!" Answers Gringin.

Genova thought of Edmund and how she'd be missing the happiest moment of his life. She may not have approved of the bride but she wanted to be there for him. The horses begun to pick up speed as Genova looked at her necklace remembering the large spark that saved her life .

"How much longer do we have till we get to where we are going?" Asks Genova.

"Two or three more days!" Says Gringin looking up from the book of Valarheyian prophecy.

Azvaskae sat on her throne which was centered in a circular clearing in the woods of Gévaudan . At her side the only thing she was allowed to take before she was banished from Valarhey. Of course the gods of Glourhaven took over so she was welcomed back anytime se wished . It was a large wolf that she called Limpy for the lopsided limp he walked with. It was a large grey wolf that Azvaskae scratched behind its ears.

The witches looked at each other as Azvaskae stood up tossing a Rock at on if them .

"How does a child best nearly fifty witches who have the upper hand in the magic system in which the shelsmyer witches draw their power ?" Asks Azvaskae.

"'She bested you too !" Says the witch that was hit with the rock .

"We need her to take off her necklace so that I can run her through with this blade !" Says Azvaskae.

"So you were able to take over an entire dimension, but you can't kill a teenager with a magic necklace!?" Asks the witch the Rock hit.

Azvaskae grabbed the witch by her Blonde hair and pulled her to her feet . The witch looked at her with fear written in her blue eyes . Azvaskae tightened her grip turning the witch into a pile of ashes.The other witches stayed quiet as Azvaskae took a seat among them brushing the ashes aside.

"Does anyone else want to remind me of my failure ?" Asks Azvaskae.

INÉS PACKED HER CLOTHES into a sack trying not to cry . It was clear her future husband had something to think about before the wedding and she needed to give time to think about it.

Edmund walked into the room snatching the wedding dress she had been folding from her hands.

"Where do you think you're going?' asks Edmund.

"My father's house I think you need to decide if you want Genova to be in your life or me !' says Inés .

Edmund tossed the dress onto his bed and looked at Inés with a face of anger. He gripped her wrists and Shook her violently . He felt wrists like putty in his hands as he shook her back and forth like a swaying timepiece.

"Your not leaving me, who do you think you are !" Shouts Edmund.

'Your hurting me stop !" Shouts Inés trying to break free of his grip.

Edmund looked at her as she begun to cry, he didn't know what had came over him. It was like he had been engulfed in an overpowering anger. Inés sat at the foot of the bed crying as her wrists began to bruise. Edmund felt every bit of his heart break, he loved Inés and didn't want to believe he was capable of doing such a thing to her.

"I'm Sorry !" Says Edmund realizing that he had done something he regretted.

it wasn't like him to do such a thing at all. He was really a kind-hearted and loving person and it made him sad to see. Edmund sat next to the crying eighteen-year-old dutchess and placed his hand on her shoulder.

'Please stay !" Says Edmund.

"I will but you can't see Genova ever again if I do!" Says Inés wiping her tears.

"YOU DON'T HAVE TO WORRY about that , she's gone away to finishing school!" Says Edmund

Genova looked at the monotonous scenery outside the window of the carriage trying not to think of how long she had until she got to Dolé and wondered what it was like. She thought of beautiful landscapes with magnificent castles guarded by thick walls of stone. Her mind began to wander back to Edmund and how she left without saying goodbye or telling him when she'd be back. He was probably worried half to death about her or probably to busy with his mind focused on the wedding to know she was gone.

Gringin looked at the young goddess who was in deep thought as she closed the book with a loud thud. A startled Genova looked at her with a face rattled with anger. Gringin smiled at her as she looked at how frightened Genova was by the closing of the book.

"You almost scared me to death!"says Genova

"Good now watch What Valarheyian magic do!" Says Gringin lifting her hand sending a ball of blue light flying through the wall of carriage in front of her.

The light flew into the air above the path in front of the horses. A portal to the entrance of a grand village lined with a stone wall at the entrance appeared in front of the horses. Genova watched as the trees outside the carriage windows turned into a bright white light that nearly blinded her. Genova's face light up with excitement as the light faded and standing next to the trees was a sign that read

"Welcome to Dolé!".

" You couldn't have done like ten hours ago ?" Asks Genova.

"I'm afraid this is where we part go to the silver scepter tavern there will find a warlock named Jean Liron!" Says Gringin opening Genova's door as the carriage came to halt.

Genova got out stretching her legs and looking to the carriage as it disappeared into a flash of light.

Genova had never been so far even the trees were different here, instead of tall pines the trees were large oaks that had dispersed their leaves onto the ground. She walked forward towards the village in the distance . The air was filled with the smells of fresh bread and sweet chocolate from the bakery that spat a thick cloud of smoke into the air. The dirt paved road that ran through the entire village. The village square was crowded with people who had been enjoying a festival . Merchants sat at their stands selling things such as precious gemstones and handmade pottery . Genova stopped and looked at a performer juggling blades as children played with wooden swords and ran about the crowd. Genova pushed her way through the crowd looking around the busy storefronts for the silver scepter tavern.

Genova saw the hanging wooden sign in the distance and made haste for the tavern. Inside the smells of ale and sweat filled the air. The barmaids delivered drinks to the paying customers as Genova looked around. It shouldn't be that hard to spot a werewolf in a place as humanly active as this establishment. Genova scanned the faces of all the men in the tavern . Each of them looked scruffy and rough . looking at them any one of them could be Jean Liron she didn't know what to do. She took a seat next to a young man who looked the same age as Edmund . He had on a red cloak pulled over his face as he looked down. Though the hood did little to hide his face or his head of long light brown hair .

"What a lovely necklace where on earth did you get it ?" Asked The boy.

Genova opened her mouth to answer the boy but realized how odd the question was as if the boy knew it was valarheyian not earthly.

"Are you Jean Lir ?"

The boy covered Genova's mouth before she could finish saying her sentence. He looked at her with anger in his eyes. It was clear the bound didn't want his identity revealed or he would have hist said yes.

"Not here too many people !" Says the boy who Genova had no doubt was Jean .

Genova looked at the boy as he took his hand from over her mouth . He took off the hood of his light brown wool spun cloak and stood up . He looked at Genova whi had become qhite frightened by the boy and his inconsiderate behavior.

"Follow me !" Says Jean .

Genova followed him out the tavern and towards the woods at the edge of the village. The two walked down the path leaving the village of Dolé behind them . Jean grabbed genova's arm and pulled her through the trees as a small stone hovel came into view. A skinny man with an unkempt beard and raggs for clothes stood outside.

"We got another witch trying, learn how to use her magic!" Says Jean

"Well out with the payment !" Says the man.

'I don't have anything to give you!" Says Genova

Then I'm afraid you'll have to rely on your coven to teach you .What are you a Gelverian witch , if so you'll be in good hands. Says the man.

"No, I am the daughter of Saren. I was sent by Zerah Shelsmyer!" Says Genova.

"She has the necklace, do you think she's telling the truth ? Asks Jean

"Of course not she's lying.,Why else do you think she came to you for help !" Says the man

walking Inside the small hovel and slamming the door closed.

Jean scratched his head looking at Genova as she looked at him with her arms folded. She didn't know why they wouldn't believe her if it was true. She had come so far and couldn't go back whence she came. Genova needed to find a way to prove she was the daughter of Saren and fast .

"Well aren't you going to tell him that it's true!" asked Genova .

"How do I know that you are her ?" Asks Jean.

Genova looked at her necklace trying to see if it would light up but it didn't. She tried focusing on the large Moon, still no light made itself appear. She snatched the necklace by the moon trying to rip it off her neck in anger but as she did a large spark flew from the crescent shaped gemstone and sent her and Jean falling flat on their backs.

"Okay I believe you now just keep your necklace on and I'll go talk to him !" Says Jean

"Why do you need his approval to teach me ?" Asks Genova.

"I don't he's the magic teacher I'm one of his students!' says Jean standing up and dusting the dirt off his pants.

He ran to the house, shutting the door gently behind him as the owl watched what was happening from the tree. It flapped its wings and flew off into the air flying over the village and high into the mountains where Nersia watched everything from afar. The owl landed on the Goddess's arm where her dress of ivy leaves wrapped around them . The owl whispered into her ear telling her what he had seen.

She was a beautiful goddess that looked as if she had been crafted from everything pure in the universe. Her skin was magnificent ebony and her hair was a beautiful shade of brown and a crown of flowers sat on top of her head. Her eyes rivaled even the greenest Emerald and her dress was made from a beautiful Green silk that had been ripped to shreds above her knees . A plethora of ivy vine covered the rest of her legs , four long stands had wrapped themselves around her arm as she listened to what the owl told her

Nersia looked at the village from on top of the mountain everything was going as she hoped all Genova had to do was learn who she truly was and the necklaCE would lose its

charm.she could blossom into the only person who could defeat
her sister. Nersia knew once she did it would only be a sort time
before her eldest sister took notice to Azvaskae's death and come
running to avenge her .

Angela was a Goddess that was going to be harder to get
rid of than Azvaskae. when she was banished Valarhey and
Glourhaven both suffered nearly a hundred years of snow. It
was what cost Valarhey the war and saved Azvaskae from being
apprehended by valarheyian troops early on in her struggle to
contain her darkness. Nersia Walked inside the damp mouth of
the cave behind her taking the owl with her on her arm as the sun
began to set behind the trees .

Edmund looked into the mirror his shirt was still on the
floor and Inés still lay half naked with nothing but her soft covers
of the bed. covering her . He looked at his hands as they begin to
shake uncontrollably.

"Are you okay ?" Asks Inés who had become frightened by
the large bite marks on her neck .

She was more concerned about why the young Marquis's
eyes were glowing a deep yellow color as he looked at himself in
the mirror .the two had been in the middle of making love when
Edmund started acting so strangely.

"I'm fine !" Replies Edmund who had grown rather alarmed
by the fact nose had begun to bleed and his mouth tasted of
blood.

"If you're fine then why are you over there when I'm all the
way over here!" Says Inés .

Edmund felt something happening Inside of him that he
couldn't explain . He fell on all fours in pain as his back begun to
contort and his bones to break. He let out a loud groan in pain as

thick reddish brown fur began to spout from his body. His nose began to grow into a long wolf-like snout and his teeth fell upon the ground.

"Edmund" asks Inés growing concerned.

She crawled forward looking to the floor where Edmund had transformed into a large Werewolf with yellow eyes that glowed like flames and a wet doglike nose. As the creature lifted itself off the ground standing on all fours it stood at five feet. A long tail wolf-like wrapped itself around Inés's arm pulling her to the ground.The creature took Edmund's likness once again and Marquis was obviously not himself his eyes still yellow and his hands were extending by long thick fingernails.

"I'm perfectly fine where we're we !" Says Edmund .

"What are you ?" asks Inés gripped in fear .

She crawled away from Edmund trying not to take her eyes off of him in fear he would tear her to shreds. Edmund looked at her in confusion; he had no recollection of what had happened .it was the price of the beast having control over him, he had no clue what was happening and what he truly was.

Chapter 4

JEAN OPENED THE DOOR as the moon lifted itself above the small hovel that spat a cloud of smoke out of the stone chimney . Genova was freezing as the cold air took pleasure in moving up the low hanging sleeves on her purple dress.

"You can keep people from killing me but you can't make any heat when I'm cold !" Genova says

as she wrapped her arms around herself to try and keep herself warm.

Jean walked over to Genova letting the door close behind him as Genova stood up .She had sat outside nearly four hours in the cold waiting for an answer.she was getting quite irritated with the whole situation.

"Well ?" Asks Genova.

"You may need to try and take off your necklace again but he said if you can prove that you are the daughter of Saren he'll teach you !" Says Jean

Genova watched as the man walked outside folding his arms in disbelief; he didn't know why the girl pretended to be something he was not. He was not only a magic teacher but a renowned Werewolf who was so skilled in magic that he was able to convince an entire village that they had burned him alive nearly two hundred years ago.

"I'm waiting!" Says The Man.

Genova yanked on the necklace and no spark came from it and the gemstone came right off.

the chain of gold keeping it on her neck. It fell on the ground and broke sending a wave of magic bursting through the forest moving the beaches of oak as it disappeared.

"Well Gilles I think you owe her an apology!" Says Jean.

"Or I could tear you both to shreds and not go through the trouble of teaching either of you!" Says the man who's name was Gilles Garnier, the infamous Werewolf of Dolé.

"He's joking, that means he just doesn't want to admit he was wrong !" Says Jean.

"Lesson number one the teacher is never wrong !" Says Giles walking back into the small stone house.

Edmund slept next to Inés with his arm wrapped around her . She lay awake looking at him in the light of the flickering candle on the nightstand next to her. She lay next to him realizing that she had found her way to one up Genova if she stayed with him through this and Genova was away at finishing school she would have done something Genova could never do. He would finally be hers like a husband was supposed to be. She still felt scared at just the thought of what she had witnessed earlier

The eighteen-year-old dutchess had not known it yet but, the child of a Werewolf was brewing Inside her waiting for the time when it could break free and continue the Fawcét bloodline of lycanthropy. Inés lifted Edmund's arm off of her and stood up, waking Edmund from a deep sleep.

He wrapped her arms around her and hugged her as she sat on the side of the bed and he dug his knees into the soft mattress.

"What's wrong ?" Asks Edmund.

"I can't sleep !" Says Inés .

Edmund kissed her neck as he tried to comfort her and she pushed him away as a great pain grew in her stomach . She screamed loudly as she began to bleed heavily in her lower regions .

Edmund opened his eyes looking at Inés as he sat up

"What's happening to you ?' asks Edmund.

Inés begun crying loudly as a small baby pushed itself out of her and Edmund picked it up . It was a boy with a coat of fur matted all over his small body. Inés fell to the ground in pain as the baby started crying.

"How is this possible?" Cried Inés .

Edmund watched as the fur disappeared and the baby lifted its small hand over his face.

Edmund looked at her and pulled himself on the bed and looked at the child with tears in her eyes. Inés was laying in a pool of crimson holding on to the last bit of life she had in her. She grabbed Edmund's wrist and looked at him with fading eyes.

"You're a werewolf my love." says Inés.

With these words she closed her eyes and died . Edmund's eyes leaked salty tears as he cradled the dead body of his wife. Edmund's Aunt walked into the room with a smile on her face. She gasped as she looked and realized the new bride was dead.

"Dear God, what happened?" Asks Edmund's Aunt.

"All I know is that thing on the bed killed her."

Edmund's Aunt Walked to the banister of the stairs and looked at the guests below. she got their attention and shouted for them all to leave. Edmund could hear the anger in her voice from the room. The baby began crying and Edmund picked him up wrapping him in the bloody sheet of the bed. The baby stopped it's crying in the arms f his father.

"We have to leave. I'll take you somewhere you'll be safe." Says Edmund's Aunt walking back into the room.

"What about the Child?" Asks Edmund.

"Take him with you." Answers Edmund's Aunt.

Edmund grabbed his brown cloak off the wooden coat rack by the door. He handed the baby to his Aunt and tied the strings of the wool cloak around his neck. He grabbed the small baby and followed his aunt to a carriage outside. Edmund's Aunt bid him farewell and with a crack of the coachman's whip Edmund left Fawcett Castle behind.

GENOVA SAT LOOKING into the bowl of gruel Giles had fixed her. She ran her spoon in the mush cereal showing her dissatisfaction with the ill-prepared meal. Jean was eating it with no problem scarfing it down like a wild dog. It was early in the morning and Genova hadn't been able to sleep well on the small cot she had been given. Her neck hurt and her back was killing her. A loud knock came from the door and Jean got up and opened the door. It was Edmund he was holding the baby in his arms and he looked at Jean trying not to cry.

"Can I help you?" Asks Jean.

"My name is Edmund Fawcett. My aunt sent me here." Says Edmund.

Genova stood up as soon as she heard Edmund's voice and rushed to the door. She opened the door and let Edmund in. Edmund's face lit up as he saw Genova.

"Did you say your name was Fawcett?" Asks Giles.

Jean fell to his knees bowing before Edmund and Giles followed suit. Genova was too stunned by the fact Edmund was holding a baby in his arms to realize that the two were practically worshiping Edmund. Genova looked at the baby in his arms trying not to let her innermost emotions show.

"You have a child." Says Genova.

"Yeah I named him Gavin, but my sweet duchess is dead." Says Edmund.

"Okay enough dilly dallying Genova Your first lesson is beginning now ." Says Giles.

Giles grabbed a strip of fabric from the cupboard and led Genova into the forest. He handed her the fabric and she looked at him. She didn't know how this piece of fabric was going to help her with magic.She examined it thoroughly and then looked back at Giles.

"For Goodness sake child, tie it around your eyes and blindfold yourself ." Shouts Giles.

GENOVA TIED THE FABRIC around her eyes and stretched her arms out in front of her. She stood up stiff and tall feeling the tree next to her. Genova tried her best to navigate the woods without falling. She took a seat on a nearby stump she had found.

"HERE'S WHAT YOU'RE going to do, you're going to use your magic to find the broomstick I have hidden in the forest. Don't come back until you've found it ." Says Giles.

"You can't expect me to actually stay out here till I find it." Says Genova.

GENOVA HEARD NOTHING in return telling her that Giles had left her alone. Genova stood up taking the blindfold off and walked deeper into the forest. As Genova walked through the woods she felt the feeling of being watched. As she looked around she saw a boy her age hiding in the trees. He had a red cloak and soft light brown skin. His hair was curly and his eyes a shimmering hazel color. He wore a white lenine shirt and a pair of black leather pants. Genova could tell he was a noble by the golden button on his cloak it had a S carved into it. The S of Saphiraun was a well-known symbol in her region because it belonged to the noble family of the neighboring fiefdom.

"WHY ARE YOU HIDING?" Asks Genova.

"I need to find Giles Garnier Somethings happened over in Gévaudan." Says the boy.

"What do you mean?" Asks Genova

"I murdered them I didn't mean to and Giles is the only one that can help me control it."

"The beast !" says the boy .

The boy turned into a ravenous monster the size of a horse. With a flat forehead and a long tasseled tail. A brownish-red

mane and eyes that shone like fire. The creature leapt on Genova
and she screamed so loudly it caught the attention of Edmund.
Edmund rushed through the woods following the screaming.
The boy turned back into his human form letting Genova go as
Edmund emerged from the trees behind them.

Genova ran back towards the house as the broomstick Giles
had hidden flew towards her. Edmund looked at the boy feeling
something inside him pulling him toward him. Edmund looked
at how scared the boy was and couldn't help but find a piece of
himself in the boy.

"You can't control it can you?" Asks Edmund.

"I need Giles Garnier to help me." Replies the boy.

"Follow me, his house is this way." Says Edmund extending
his hand.

The two walked back to Giles's hovel and Edmund let the
boy inside. Jean handed Gavin to Edmund and Genova sat at
the wooden table. She had found the broomstick or rather it had
found her in her state of fear. That seemed to be the only time
she was able to make magic happen.

Far away from the small hovel Azvaskae had retired to her
Castle high up in the mountains. She was in her lair which was
in the tallest tower of the menacing black stone fortress. She
was cooking up a creation that would help her find Genova. A
vampire that would appear human she had already created two
races of vampires when she was taking over the Ferahogan Solar
system but now she'd unleash a new race on the earth .

Azvaskae stood above a bubbling cauldron that was alive
with purple and black smoke. She took a vial from the podium
she had set in front of the boiling iron pot. She ran her finger
down the page of the book of Glourhaven spells. Not that she

needed it she was after all the Queen of Glourhaven. Which was the regime of Gods that had dethroned the Faun King Saren.

"The last ingredient to make the male a drop of blood from a bat's tail. Boil cauldron and boil well for when all is mixed you shall cast my spell. One thousand men of vampiric nature who thrive on drinking blood arise from my cauldron." Says Azvaskae.

A bolt of lightning struck the cauldron and Azvaskae covered her face with her long flowing sleeves. From the boiling pot flew a thousand bats that turned into men of all different skin colors. Azvaskae took a pink vial of glowing liquid and tossed it's content into the bubbling pot. The cauldron sent forth another thousand bats this time they turned into female vampires.

"My sanguinarians go forth and find the maiden with golden brown skin and brown locks of fine silk. The moon Goddess of valarhey and when you do bring her to me." Says Azvaskae.

The vampires all turned into bats and took off leaving their creator behind. Back at Giles's hovel night had fallen and Edmund couldn't sleep. The little baby was fast asleep next to Genova who was also sleeping. Edmund looked across the room to the bed of the boy he had shown the way to the small hovel. He noticed that he wasn't in the bed or inside the cottage. Edmund propped himself up looking around. He climbed out of bed and walked outside he saw the boy sitting on a log. Edmund sat on the log and looked up at the stars.

"You can't sleep either?" Asks Edmund.

"I haven't slept in over a month." Says The boy.

"My name is Edmund" Says Edmund extending his hand.

"Eloijah." Says The boy as he shook his hand.

"So you're a werewolf too?" Asks Edmund.

"No, worse I'm a werelion." Says Eloijah.

"Are you the beast that's been ripping people apart in Gévaudan?" Asks Edmund.

"Yes but I don't want to be." Answered Eloijah as he started to cry.

Edmund felt the same as him; he wanted to be able to control the beast that ran through his veins. He looked at the boy who was beginning to cry and found himself in more ways than one. It was heartbreaking to see him cry s Edmund offered him his shoulder. Eloijah cried his heart out on it as Edmund looked up at the stars. The two talked all night letting their minds wander freely. Soon the sun began to rise and the two realized just how long they'd been outside.

Genova walked outside carrying Gavin in her hands. Her hair had been tied back and her necklace had been fixed. Genova only hoped that her magic was powerful enough to restore the enchantment that had saved her life. She handed Gavin to Edmund and walked towards the woods .

"Where are you going ?" Asks Edmund.

"To town, I need some real food." Says Genova.

Edmund and Eloijah followed Genova to town.Leaving behind the shabby hovel. Genova thought of what the future would hold and how she needed to learn how to use her powers fairly quickly. With her new friends Genova felt like it was truly possible.

Part 2 The king of Werewolves and The Prince Of Werelions

Chapter 5

GENOVA SAT IN THE TAVERN she had met Jean in downing a pint of beer. Edmund and Eloijah seemed to be getting along well. Genova took notice to The handsome nobleman who sat across the room eying her. He was a handsome man with golden hair and deep blue eyes . Genova dowed her pint as te young NobeGenova walked outside carrying Gavin in her hands. Her hair had been tied back and her necklace had been fixed. Genova only hoped that her magic was powerful enough to restore the enchantment that had saved her life. She handed Gavin to Edmund and walked towards the woods ."Where are you going ?" Asks Edmund."To town, I need some real food." Says Genova.Edmund nnd Eloijah followed Genova to town.Leaving behind the shabby hovel. Genova thought of what the future would hold and how she needed to learn how to use her powers fairly quickly. With her new friends Genova felt like it was truly possible.

Part 2 The king of Werewolves and The Prince Of Werelions

Chapter 6

GENOVA SAT IN THE TAVERN she had met Jean in downing a pint of beer. Edmund and Eloijah seemed to be getting along well. Genova took notice to The handsome nobleman who sat across the room eying her. He was a handsome man with golden hair and deep blue eyes . Genova dowed her pint as the young nobel walked toward her.

"Can I get you another drink?" Asks The Nobleman.

Genova looked at Edmund as he slipped out the tavern with Eloijah. Maybe she needed to forget about the young Marquis. Genova looked back at the nobleman and nodded. He snapped his fingers and two pints were brought to him. He handed one to Genova and took the other for himself. He took a seat in front of Genova and reached for her hand. Genova pulled her hand away and tried her best to feel uncomfortable.

"You know what I think i'm just going to go." Says Genova standing up.

Edmund and Eloijah walked through the woods and edmund couldn't help but feel he was right where he was meant to be. Eloijah was everything if not more than he could as for in a partner , but edmund knew he could never tell the young werelion. Still Edmund liked to feel the rush of being near him.

Edmund looked at Eloijah trying his best not to blush but his face went red as a cherry.

"TONIGHT IS THE HALF moon I'll be turning tonight so i think it's best if i'm far way from you guys." Says Eloijah.

"Let me come with you please ." Edmund.

"Edmund you don't know what i'm capable of." replies Eloijah.

"I don't care we are the same and you need someone who understands you." Says Edmund.

The two walked and as they did Edmund reached for Eloijah's hand. He held it and the two walked the forest together. Edmund laid his head on Elijah's shoulder and Eloijah smiled. Maybe just maybe he felt the same way.

GENOVA WALKED INTO the hovel and heard the baby crying. She picked him up and he stopped. Genova cradled the baby in her arms. She looked at the baby and smiled. She wanted desperately to be a mother one day and now she would have experience for when she was one.

"Shh little one you're okay." Says Genova.

Genova set the baby on Edmund's bed as Edmund walked in . She noticed Eloijah wasn't with him, But Edmund's face had was lit up like a torch. He blushed and smiled like Genova had never seen before.

"What's gotten you in such a good mood?" Asks Genova.

"I think I'm in love."says Edmund.

Genova needed to hear Edmund say it, she already knew who he was in love with. She needed to hear it so she could move on and try to let go of this unhealthy obsession she had with Edmund. She knew she'd never be anything more than his friend. Genova had come to grips with it and now she needed to hear him confirm it.

"With who?" Asks Genova with a fake laugh.

"Eloijah." Says Edmund.

Genova's heart shattered but her emotions were able to piece it back together this time. She wasn't sad nor mad in fact the young Goddess was happy. At least that's what she wanted to happen. Genova fought her tears as she walked outside grabbing the necklace off her bed on the way out. Giles had fixed it goe her and now she was able to go about without being accompanied by someone else.

Genova sat on stump she had found when she was waiting for Jean. She could say and cried knowing now she had wasted so many years wishing for something that would never be. The Heartbroken Goddess cried her eyes off as she sat on the stump. Her necklace begun to glow a silver color as she cried. Genova wiped her eyes and looked at the necklace.

The silver light sparkled blinking with a majestic shimmer. The wind picked up and the leaves that had fallen off the trees lifted into the air. The leaves formed a faun with a muscular build.

"Do not be afraid, my sweet little girl. For it me your father Saren." Says the faun made of leaves.

"This is your fault, why did you send me here . You sent me away, you abandoned me and now because of you I'm heartbroken."says Genova starting to crying.

"My dear child I'm sorry for the pain I have caused you but know that every bit of it I would put you through again for the return of the light. Your human experience is what you need to endure in order to defeat my niece. You are the light but you can not defeat her unless you learn to harness your gifts." Says the faun made of leaves.

THE DOOR OPENED AND Edmund walked out causing the leaves to fall back to the ground. Genova's necklace stopped flashing as Edmund walked towards her.

"I need your help Genova." Says Edmund.

"With what ?" Asks Genova.

"I want you to make the fireflies dance around when I tell Eloijah I want to be with him." Says Edmund.

Genova wanted to refuse but Edmund looked so happy. She wanted him to be happy even if it hurt her. So she nodded and smiled even though she was dying on the inside. She didn't exactly know of she could make fire

"How am I going to do that ?" Asks Genova.

"Just try please." Says Edmund.

Not too far away in the woods Eloijah walked through the woods and stopped at a tree with a slit in it's trunk. He grabbed the book he placed in the tree earlier and flipped through the pages. He stopped on a page titled unlove spell. It was a song that would make Edmund not feel the way he did about him.

"I PUT A SPELL ON YOU Edmund Fawcett I truly do.

I release you of my hold on you.

You better stop the things You're doing. I ain't lying

I put a spell on you You'll never be mine.

I can't love you the way you want me to.

I'll never give my heart to you!" Sang Eloijah.

His voice carried in the wind as it picked up blowing his long curly brown hair. Eloijah began dancing round and round . His voice bounced around him with magic echoes. He flipped the pages as his eyes begun to light up with a yellow light.

"I PUT A SPELL ON YOU My dear werewolf king And I ain't lying.

There's no room in the world For the love of a Werewolf and a Werelion.

I put a spell on you , I release you of my hold on you.

You better stop the things You're doing. I ain't lying

I put a spell on you You'll never be mine." Continued Eloijah.

A large flash of light burst from the book and Eloijah's echoes ran through the forests. His eyes returned to their normal light brown color. The book closed as the spell ended and Eloijah hid it in the tree again. He walked back towards the hovel he had departed from earlier.

Eloijah had done something horrible he knew that was certain. He couldn't have Edmund falling in love with him. If he was ever going to learn how to control the lion that was killing so many people he didn't have time for love so even though he felt the same way he had done what he needed to.

CHAPTER 7

GENOVA SAT IN A BRANCH high up in a tree near Giles's house waiting for Eloijah to come. The sun had already faded giving way to a night lit by a crescent moon. She heard Eloijah humming the spell he had done earlier as he approached. Genova, fairly certain she had mastered how to use her magic, a tiny bit wiggled her fingers causing the door of the hovel to open and Edmund walked out wearing a clean green jacket with golden buttons. He had on a hat with a large light pink feather coming from it and a pair of black leather pants with a pair of black boots.

Genova moved her pointer finger in a circular motion causing a great swarm of fireflies to circle the two. Eloijah's spell didn't work because Genova had gone above and beyond to make sure that Eloijah and Edmund were together she had manifested and set her intentions. She could see Eloijah resisting so she closed her thumb and pointer finger together causing the fireflies to bring them closer together. Giles stood in the door way playing a romantic piece on the violin.

ELOIJAH NEARED EDMUND, letting him kiss him. Genova could get a small glimpse from the branch she sat on. She thought it would fill her with rage but it actually made her happy to see that they were happy. The beautiful moment was just that, a moment. Genova saw Eloijah fall to the ground and she knew that meant his lion was taking over. She jumped down from the tree and helped him up . She helped him walk away from the hovel and back into the forest.

"YOU'RE GOING TO BE okay." Says Genova.

"No you need to leave?" Says Eloijah pulling away from her.

Genova watched as he fell onto his hands and knees and transformed into a large beast with a tasseled tail. The air around Genova grew cold as the creature stood up on all fours revealing it 0p nearly six feet tall in height. It looked back at Genova revealing a flat forehead and a large snarling mouth.Genova screamed as the creature turned to her lifting one of it's massive paws.

GENOVA WAITED FOR THE impact but when it didn't come she looked up and saw ty lion wasn't targeting her. A Sanguinarian vampire had come from the trees and tried to attack Genova. The lion tackled it and Genova looked in fear as two batlike creatures came and lifted the poor Werelion away. She knew right away they worked for her cousin. She ran back to the hovel and saw Giles wasn't there but Edmund held the baby in his arms.

"They took him we have to go." Says Genova.

"Who did they take?" Asks Edmund.

"Eloijah!" Says Genova.

Edmund handed Gavin to Genova and rushed outside; he saw that the vampires were carrying Eloijah away. He ran after them deep into the woods running with everything he had inside him. It no use they carried the Werelion far away from the hovel. The vampires dropped Eloijah in front of Azvaskae. Her face was lit up with a smile that soon faded as she realized they didn't bring her Genova.

"What is this. I told you to bring me Genova not one of her werepets." Says Azvaskae.

The lion turned back into Eloijah as dawn approached.

"I'm no one's pet!" Says Eloijah.

"This may be able to work to our advantage. Eloijah I know who you are the great beast of Gévaudan. So either tell me where Genova is or die." Says Azvaskae.

"How could you kill me ?" Asks Eloijah.

"Not me the people of Gévaudan and the countless other villages you have ravaged." Laughs Azvaskae.

"I'll never tell you where she is." Says Eloijah.

"Suit yourself." Says Azvaskae.

Azvaskae walked into the forest and the vampires guarded Eloijah. Eloijah stood up and looked around he knew exactly where he was. He was in the forest of Gévaudan. Azvaskae had planned for them to bring him here. He was going to die today and Eloijah was ready for it. It was the only fate befitting a monster that had caused so much carnage.

It wasn't long before Azvaskae returned with a large mob of villagers who had lit torches and pitchforks in their hands. Some held wooden clubs others held large swords and some even held guns.

"The great Werelion of Gévaudan." Says Azvaskae.

FAR AWAY IN THE HOVEL Genova and Edmund watched what was happening to Eloijah through a large bubbling cauldron. Edmund walked away from the cauldron and to the the bookshelf of spellbooks. He pulled out a protection spell book and flipped through the pages. Giles walked through the door and looked at Genova.

"We have to go I've secured passage for you two out of France." Says Giles.

I'm not going anywhere

"Her vampires are already on the way." Says Giles.

"I don't care I won't let them hurt him!" Shouts Edmund.

Giles and Genova drug Edmund towards the door. The two tried all their strength and finally got him out the hovel. A carriage waited outside they put Edmund inside and got in. The carriage took off and Genova felt a sense of somber familiarity to this situation. It was the same way she had let her mother die. She knew that Gécaudan was on the way to the harbor and she intended on saving her friend. She wasn't about to let another one of her friends die because of her.

Chapter 8

THE VILLAGERS BEAT Eloijah with clubs and he screamed as his bones broke. He shouted as another person took a blow at him. His eyes filled let tears fall and his face was stained with blood from the pitchfork that had stayed the side of his face.

"She's in the house of the werewolf of Dolé !" Shouts Eloijah.

Azvaskae snapped her fingers and Eloijah was replaced with a person that looked like him. Eloijah appeared at a tavern where a band of slave traders took him captive. The villagers beat the look alike and tied him up to a tree. There they piled dried leaves and pieces of dead shrubs at his feet. Genova and Edmund watched from a tree as the look alike was set ablaze. Unaware of what had happened Edmund screamed with sadness but Genova covered his mouth.

"Let the Great Werelion burn!" Shouts Azvaskae.

A villager holding a torch set the pile of dried leaves and shrubs ablaze. Edmund cried and Genova helped him back to the carriage. Genova couldn't help but feel defeated. How could she stop such a evil creature? She looked out the window as the carriage rushed away from the village of Gévaudan.

"WHERE ARE WE GOING?" Asks Genova.

"Do you remember your cousin Nicholas?" Asks Giles.

"Yes but I haven't seen him in years." Says Genova.

"He's offered you safe haven in his court." Says Giles.

How will I learn how to harness my gifts

"In Moderjord you'll be sent with more than enough supplies and in your things you'll find a book that will tell you the last deed you need to complete before you're ready to harness them." Says Giles.

"What if I can't?" Asks Genova.

"You have to Genova or else Eloijah died in vain." Says Edmund.

The carriage pulled up to the harbor and Edmund and Genova got out. They didn't notice Eloijah getting loaded onto a slave ship along with a group of other Africans. The got into their ship and it set sail. Genova knew she would miss France but she glad she was getting away from Azvaskae. Genova let the early morning air blow her long curly brown hair as she watched the land drift further and further away m She wondered what Nicholas would look like the young prince would be twenty soon so he wouldn't be the same twelve year old she had seen years ago.

"SHALL I SHOW YOU TO your room your grace?" Asks one of the crew members.

Genova followed him to the lower decks and he lead her to a large room with a porthole window. In the center was a large canopy bed with vibrant pink curtains.Near the bed was two large bags which she knew were the things Giles had arranged for her to bring. Genova laid on the bed and tried her best to get some rest and Edmund knocked on the door Genova answered it and saw Edmund holding Gavin.

"He wants his aunt Genova." Says Edmund.

GENOVA TOOK THE BABY from Edmund and saw the small werewolf baby smile at her. At least she still had Edmund and Gavin. Genova thought it was bitter sweet that Edmund was the one part of her life that would stay the same . He was there through everything and even if it wasn't as her lover she was happy. Edmund walked in Genova's room and closed the door.

"I'm sorry that I can't love you in the way you want me to." Says Edmund.

"What ?" Asks Genova.

"I know you love me as a lover but I don't want to lose you. Everyone I've ever loved is dead and I can't lose you too." Says Edmund.

"Edmund I love you more than you know but all I want is your happiness." Says Genova.

Edmund kissed her on the cheek and left the room leaving her with closure she needed for so long. Genova smiled as she laid on the bed with Gavin next to her. She closed her eyes for the first time in a while she slept. How fitting it was that the Goddess Of The Moon Slept during the day. There she slept till she arrived in the kingdom of Moderjord four days later.

THE END

Did you love *The Genova Chronicles : Goddess Of The Moon*? Then you should read *The Lycanthrope Confessions*[1] by J.N. Macawell!

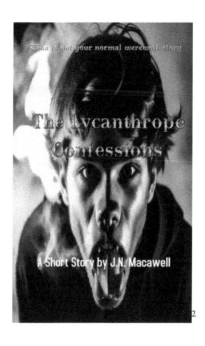

The Lycanthrope Confessions tells the story of 17 year old Jacob Liron and his quest to be cured of a curse that he accidentally placed upon himself. Can Jacob free himself or will he be stuck turning into a werewolf every night

---

1. https://books2read.com/u/4DD2y7

2. https://books2read.com/u/4DD2y7

Also by J.N. Macawell

Grim Kid
Grim kid new world order
Grim Kid: Son Of The Grim Reaper

Grim kid stories
Aidan The Devil's Cambion : A Grim Kid Story
Woe Of The Nephilim
ADONIJAH : A Grim Kid story

Mythical tales
Moonlit A Werewolf's Tale
Broomstick a witch's tale

The Abaddon Chronicles
1692

The Genova chronicles
The Genova Chronicles : Goddess Of The Moon

Wizards and Genies
Wizards And Genies: The Prince Of Arevesa

Standalone
Seasick A Merman's Tale Part 1
The Lycanthrope Confessions
The Skinwalker
The Snow Queen By J.N. Macawell
SeaSick A merman's Tale part 2
Stumpp The Werewolf Of Bedburg
Reaper An Angel's Tale
The skudakumooch
Star Child

Milton Keynes UK
Ingram Content Group UK Ltd.
UKHW021826031123
431730UK00011B/107

9 798223 574026